For Nicholas
—M.K.

Daddy's Little Boy
Words and music copyright © 1950, 1978 by Cherio Corp.
Illustrations copyright © 2004 by Maggie Kneen
Manufactured in China by South China Printing Company Ltd.
www.harperchildrens.com

Library of Congress Cataloging-in-Publication Data
Collins, Billy.
  Daddy's little boy / words and music by Billy Collins ; pictures
by Maggie Kneen.—1st ed.
    p.   cm.
  Summary: An illustrated version of a song which describes
how special a son is to his father.
  ISBN 0-06-029003-X
  1. Children's songs, English—Texts. [1. Fathers and sons—Songs
and music. 2. Songs.] I. Kneen, Maggie., ill. II. Title.
PZ8.3.C6825Dad 2004
782.42164'0268—dc21
                                                              2003008335

Typography by Jeanne L. Hogle
1 2 3 4 5 6 7 8 9 10
❖
First Edition

Daddy's Little Boy

Words and music by Billy Collins
Pictures by Maggie Kneen

HarperCollins Publishers

 ou're an angel from heaven, sent down from above,

You're Daddy's little boy to have and to love;

Boy of mine, you're a fine little laddie,
You're the world to your Mommy and Daddy;

You're a good little soldier who always obeys,

You bring me happiness in so many ways;

You're as cute as a toy,
You're my pride and joy,

And you're Daddy's little boy.

All the world and its gold couldn't buy you from me,

With Daddy's little boy, I'm rich as can be;

With your smile, you make life worthwhile living,

And you make every day my Thanksgiving;

You're my proudest possession, a gem from above,

You're all the precious things that dreams are made of;

When you grow up like me,
You'll still always be,
Just your daddy's little boy.

DADDY'S LITTLE BOY

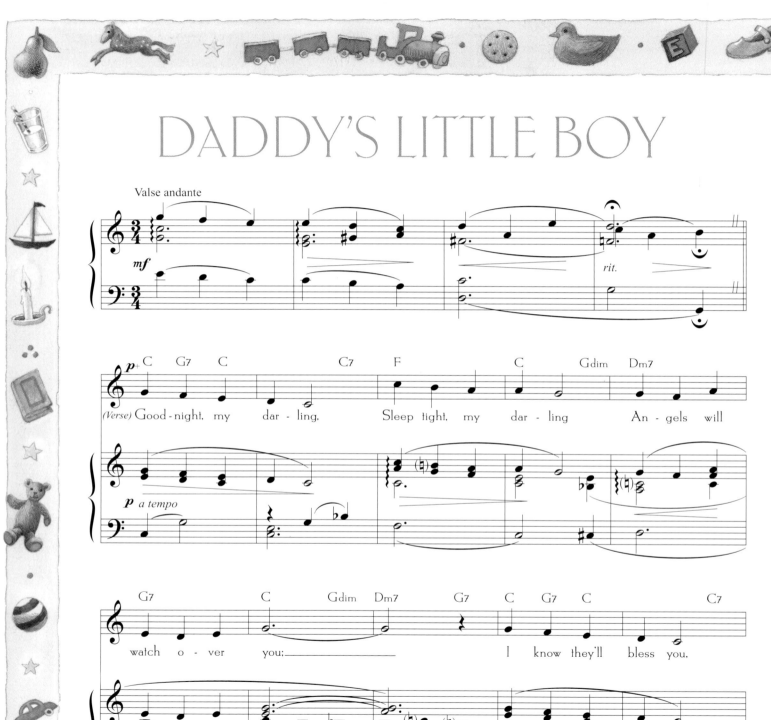

Valse andante

mf

rit.

p C   G7   C   C7   F   C   Gdim   Dm7

(Verse) Good-night, my   dar - ling,   Sleep tight, my   dar - ling   An - gels will

p a tempo

G7   C   Gdim Dm7   G7   C   G7   C   C7

watch o - ver   you;_____   I   know they'll   bless you,

Kiss and ca - ress you, They love you as much as I do:___

CHORUS *(Tenderly)*

1. You're an an - gel from heav - en, sent down from a -
(2. All the) world and its gold could - n't buy you from

bove, You're DAD - DY'S LIT - TLE BOY to have and to
me, With DAD - DY'S LIT - TLE BOY, I'm rich as can